# RAY

MARIANNA COPPO

tundra

At the end of the hall,
near the staircase,
there's a closet.

Inside lives Ray.

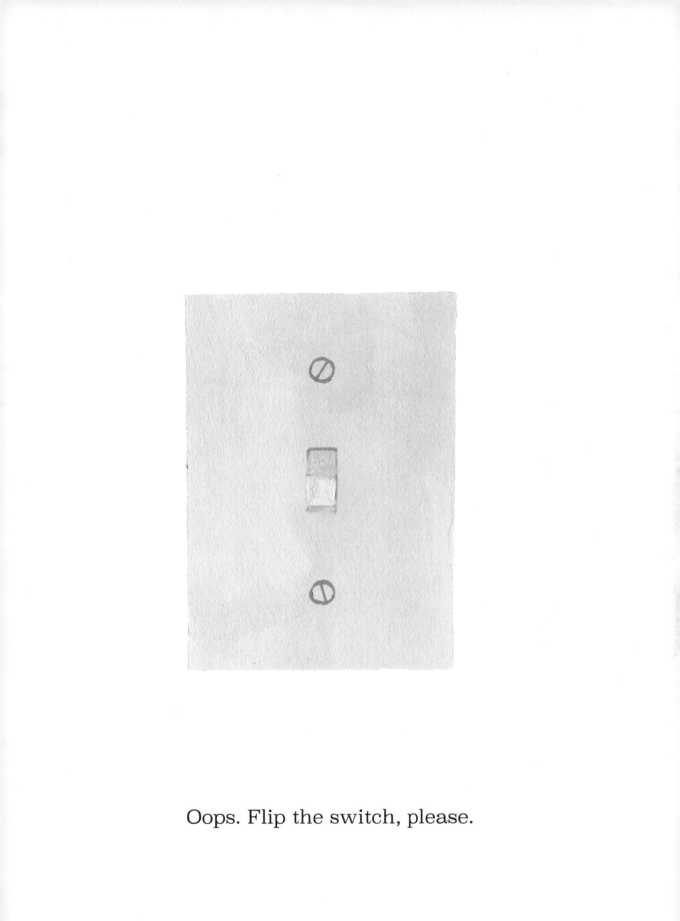

Oops. Flip the switch, please.

That's better.
So, this is Ray.

Ray has seen better days.

And worse ones too.

But now this is his home.
It isn't much. The closet
goes from here to there.
That's it.

Inside there are all sorts of things.

When he's bored (rather often), Ray counts them.

Once he counted as many as 41 things.

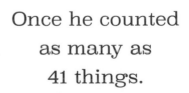

Ray's favorite things
are book covers,

Tom the spider,

and secret hideouts.

The closet, the things
and even Tom the spider
often disappear.

Ray does not like this.

Darkness is boring
if you don't know
how to fill it.

So boring that Ray usually slips into
a dreamless sleep.

Time goes by and
things change.

But not very much.

Then,
one day,
Ray feels his
head spin.

He feels upside down.

And then
strangely light.

The closet is gone.
In its place, there is
another place.

Ray can't tell where it
begins or where it ends.

He tries counting what he sees,
but there are just too many things.

(And Ray
can only
count to 41.)

He recognizes
some things:

Christmas trees
(not one, but many),

a very long scarf,

and a giant vase.

(Sadly, no sign of
Tom the spider.)

But everything is big,
super big.

And Ray has never
felt so small.

Everyone is asleep now.

Except for Ray.

For once,
he has something
better to do.

Look, a shooting star.
Make a wish.

Ray has just made one too.
(Obviously, I can't tell you
what he wished for.)

The moment Ray finally falls asleep,

something happens.

When he wakes
up, right there in
front of him,

shines the biggest
light bulb in the
world.

Ray is glowing.

The closet is right
where we left it.
(Only Tom the
spider has moved.)

Everything is
exactly the same.

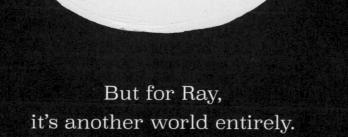

But for Ray,
it's another world entirely.